P9-DTO-827

For Brad, who taught me to love robots.
—K. K. O.

For Colette, Tom, and Adam.
—K. S.

STERLING CHILDREN'S BOOKS
New York

An Imprint of Sterling Publishing Co., Inc.
1166 Avenue of the Americas
New York, NY 10036

Sterling Children's Books and the distinctive Sterling Children's Books logo
are registered trademarks of Sterling Publishing Co., Inc.

Text © 2017 Karen Kaufman Orloff
Illustrations © 2017 Kim Smith

ISBN 978-1-4549-2118-9

Distributed in Canada by Sterling Publishing Co., Inc.
c/o Canadian Manda Group, 664 Annette Street
Toronto, Ontario, Canada M6S 2C8
Distributed in the United Kingdom by GMC Distribution Services
Castle Place, 166 High Street, Lewes, East Sussex, England BN7 1XU
Distributed in Australia by NewSouth Books
45 Beach Street, Coogee, NSW 2034, Australia

For information about custom editions, special sales, and premium and corporate purchases,
please contact Sterling Special Sales at 800-805-5489 or specialsales@sterlingpublishing.com.

Manufactured in China

Lot #:
2 4 6 8 10 9 7 5 3 1
07/17

sterlingpublishing.com

The artwork for this book was created digitally.
Design by Ryan Thomann

GoodNight, Little Bot

by **Karen Kaufman Orloff**   illustrated by **Kim Smith**

STERLING CHILDREN'S BOOKS
New York

Little Bot, it's time for bed.
Let's get ready, sleepyhead.

Put down the game.
Turn off TV.
It's almost bedtime,
can't you see?

Don't say "No," and don't protest.
Little robots need their rest.

Roll your wheels into the tub.
Shine your metal. Scrub, scrub, scrub!

PJs over power pack.

Batteries—
a tasty snack.

Sipping oil, nice and slow,
helps to make a robot grow.

Still so energized
and wired!

Little Bot—
why aren't you tired?

Comb your circuits.

Brush your bolts.

Plug you in.
Recharge your volts.

Reading time.
A cozy spot.
A bedtime book
for little Bot.

Ten more books? That's quite a few.
How about I just read two?

Stay in bed, now, don't get wild.
Power down, sweet robot child.

I know it's hard to fall asleep.

Let's try counting robot sheep.

Check for monsters under bed.

Sensors quiet.

Lay your head.

A blankie tuck.

A hug to share.

A kiss for Botty Teddy Bear.

Lullaby.

Pull covers tight.

A little bot . . .

. . . down for the night.